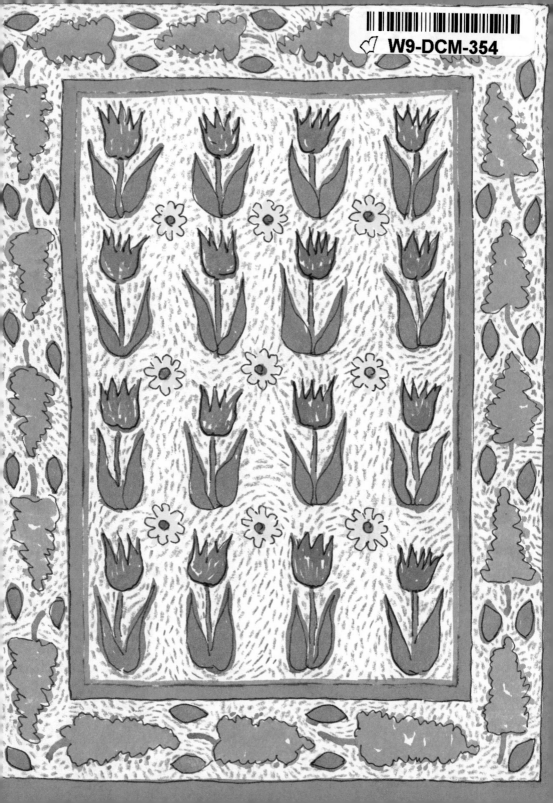

TO MY MOTHER, WHO STALKS THE PAGES
OF ALL MY STORIES – J.D.

FOR MARC GAVE – M.B.

Library of Congress Cataloging in Publication Data

Delton, Judy
  Rabbit's new rug.

  SUMMARY: Rabbit loves his beautiful new rug,
but comes to realize there are more important things.
  [1. Friendship—Fiction. 2. Rabbits—Fiction]
I. Brown, Marc Tolon. II. Title
PZ7.D388Rac   [E]   79–16639
ISBN 0–8193–1009–3 ISBN 0–8193–1010–7 lib. bdg.

JUDY DELTON
RABBIT'S
NEW RUG

PICTURES BY MARC BROWN

PARENTS MAGAZINE PRESS · NEW YORK

Rabbit had a new rug in his house.
The Flora Floor Store had just
delivered it.
The rug had large red tulips on it,
and small yellow daisies.
It had green leaves and
light blue snapdragons.

Rabbit clapped his paws together.
"My new rug is so pretty,
I'll call my friends over to see it."

Rabbit dialed Fox's number.

"I'll be over as soon as my strawberry jam is cooked," he said.

Then rabbit called Owl.

"I'll come as soon as I finish my nap," he said sleepily, looking at his watch.

Rabbit was waiting at his door
for his friends.

When Fox arrived, he looked over
Rabbit's shoulder at the new rug.
"What a beautiful rug!" he said.
"What fine-looking red flowers.
Red is my favorite color, you know."
Fox began to walk into the house.

"Walk along the edges of the room, then,"
said Rabbit. "Just don't step on the rug."
Fox sighed and squeezed close to the wall.
"I hope you wiped your feet on the mat,"
scolded Rabbit. "You really should have
worn your galoshes in this weather."

"Rabbit! It is summer! No one wears
galoshes in summer! Here, I brought
a jar of jam for you."

"Thank you, Fox. But we'd better not open it. Some might get on my rug, and leave a terrible, sticky spot."

"It wouldn't show if it fell on the red flowers," said Fox under his breath.

Soon Owl came to the door.
He handed Rabbit a plate of brownies.
"From the bakery," he yawned.
"I wanted to bring a treat and I didn't
have time to bake so early in the day."

"Early!" said Fox. "It is two o'clock —
the day is half over."

"Not for me," said Owl.
"It hasn't even begun yet."

"Thank you for the brownies, Owl,"
said Rabbit.
"But we had better not eat them.
Someone might spill crumbs
on my new rug."

Owl looked at the rug.
"That is a fine rug, Rabbit.
Almost too pretty to walk on."

"That's why I'm standing here
near the wall," muttered Fox.

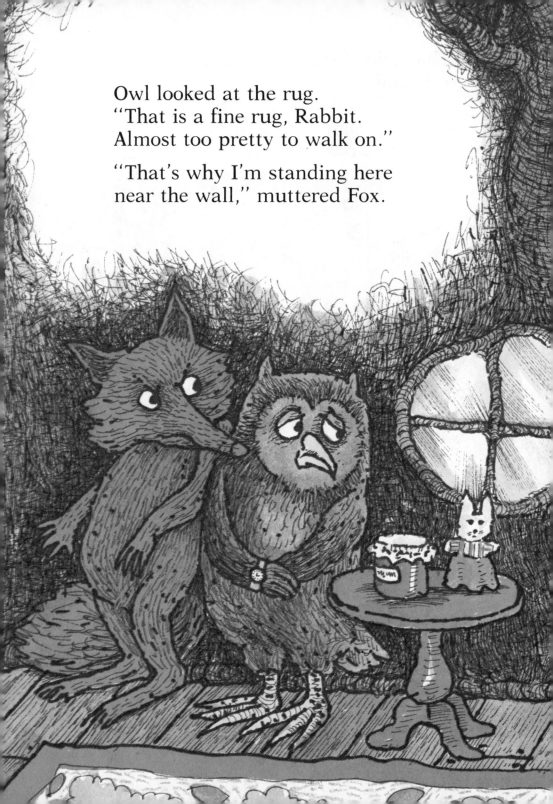

Just then Raccoon came by,
and looked in the door.
"Why, Rabbit! You have a new rug!"
he said. Then he noticed his
friends leaning up against the wall.

Raccoon wondered why they were standing there.
But before he could say anything, Rabbit asked,
"Are you molting, Raccoon?"
"Black hair would look bad on this new rug."

"No, no, I'm not molting," said Raccoon.
"I think BIRDS molt," he said, frowning at Owl.

The animals stood in a row along the wall
and admired Rabbit's new rug.

"The flowers look real enough to pick," said Fox.
"The sun makes them sparkle," said Owl.
"It's such a cheerful rug," said Rabbit happily.
"Perhaps we should leave," murmured Raccoon.

The animals filed out the door.
"Good-by!" called Rabbit.

The next day Rabbit admired his rug
all day long. He felt how soft it was.
He vacuumed and brushed it three times.
He used his carpet sweeper twice.

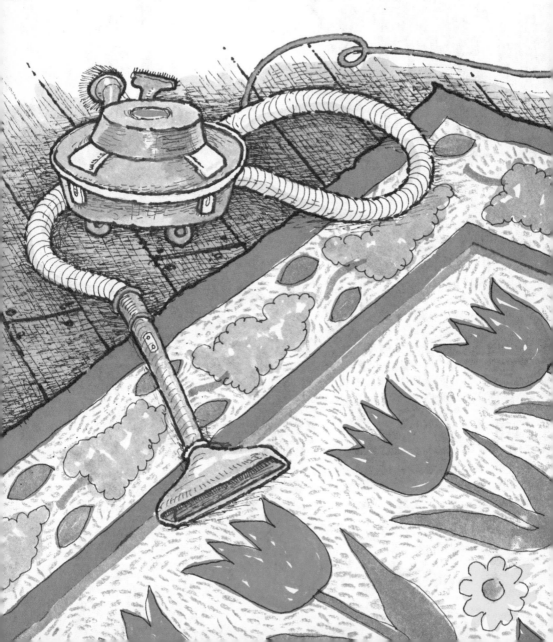

"What a handsome rug," he said to himself.
"I have never seen another like it.
No one in the woods has such a colorful one."

Every day Rabbit admired his rug.
Every day he walked around the rug
so he wouldn't make footprints on it.

And every day he was alone.
No one came to see him.
A week went by.
One morning, Rabbit said to himself,
"It sure is quiet around here.
I would bake, but I may
get flour on my rug.
I would sew, but threads and lint
would fall all over it."

The hours grew longer and longer.
Rabbit had read all of his books
and he was tired of watching TV.
Tears came to his eyes.
"A rug isn't much company," he said.
"I miss my friends."

The next day, Rabbit called Fox
and Owl and Raccoon on the telephone.
"I am having a party this afternoon,"
he said to each of them.

"I would like you to come."
"A party?" they each said in surprise.
"Ha, that should be fun," thought Fox.
"All of us squeezing next to the wall."

Meanwhile, Rabbit hung balloons
and streamers in his living room
and put flowers on the table.
He planned games, and bought prizes
for the winners.

At two o'clock the animals arrived
at Rabbit's house. Fox looked suspicious.
Raccoon looked doubtful. Owl looked sleepy.
Fox knocked on the door.
"Maybe the party is in the yard,"
said Raccoon, looking around.

Just then, Rabbit opened the door.
"Come in," he said happily.
"I'm so glad to see you."

"But," said Fox, "what about your new rug?"
"What about it?" said Rabbit.
"Does that mean we can walk on it?"
asked Raccoon.

Rabbit nodded.
"Well, I'll be," said Owl, rubbing his eyes.
And so they all went inside.

The friends sang, "Old MacDonald had a farm . . ."
and played Pin the Tail on the Donkey.
They laughed and talked and then
they ate pie and cake and nuts and candy.
Rabbit did not say anything when
crumbs fell on the rug.

"What a great party!" said Fox.
"What good food!" said Raccoon.
"It's a fine new-rug celebration,"
said Owl, who was wide awake now.

After everyone left,
Rabbit sat in his rocking chair.
He rocked back and forth on his new rug.
He looked at the bright flowers.
All around him he saw streamers
and balloons and leftover food.
Rabbit yawned and then he smiled.
"There's nothing like old friends
to help break in a new rug," he said.

ABOUT THE AUTHOR

JUDY DELTON is a busy writer and teacher. Besides her dozen books for children, she has written many articles and essays. Before she raised her family, she taught elementary school. And now she teaches writing in colleges and on her own. From her home in St. Paul, Minnesota, she travels around the Midwest as a favorite speaker and leader of writing workshops.

She says, "Many of the characters in my picture books are based on people in my life. For example, Rabbit in RABBIT'S NEW RUG reminds me of my mother, who, when I was a child, had me take my shoes off on the porch so I wouldn't 'track up the rug.'"

ABOUT THE ARTIST

MARC BROWN says, "RABBIT'S NEW RUG is the kind of story I would write myself. I saw the characters as I read it for the first time. All the animals are like people I know."

Besides drawing pictures for other people's writing, Mr. Brown does illustrate his own books, too, which have been published by several companies. He works at a big table in an old house just a stone's throw from the harbor of Hingham, Massachusetts, where he's often distracted by his two young sons and other growing things.

PARENTS MAGAZINE PRESS welcomes both Judy Delton and Marc Brown to its list for the first time.